Praise for the *Kingdom of Silk* series:

'A truly beautiful story of loss, hope, strength and love...unforgettable.'

'Poignant and lovely... of ...aking you feel ... own ...ese characters, and this place, always.'
Daniel Hahn, *The Independent on Sunday*

'Rarely has a series of books had such an effect on me. Never have I felt such yearning to be part of a fictional family. Never have I cried both of sorrow and elation as much as I have with every single book this series. It really is a magnificent series.'
Mélanie McGilloway, *Library Mice*

'If you haven't heard of the *Kingdom of Silk* books then it's high time you discovered them.'
Alison Potter, *Junior Magazine*

'A beautifully crafted story... Glenda Millard has a genius for letting the plot unfold.'
Ann Lazim, *Centre for Literacy in Primary Education*

'A special, lyrical and lovely story... It will surely touch your heart.' *Berlie Doherty*

'Guaranteed to delight all generations of the family.'
Lancashire Evening Post

The *Kingdom of Silk* series:

PLUM PUDDINGS AND PAPER MOONS

by Glenda Millard

Illustrated by Stephen Michael King

Plum Puddings and Paper Moons

ISBN: 978-1-907912-31-3

First published in Australia in 2008 by ABC Books for the Australian
Broadcasting Corporation.

This edition first published in the UK by Phoenix Yard Books Ltd, 2014.
Published by arrangement with Rights People, London.

Phoenix Yard Books
Phoenix Yard
65 King's Cross Road
London WC1X 9LW
www.phoenixyardbooks.com

1 3 5 7 9 10 8 6 4 2

A catalogue record for this book is available from the British Libray

Contents

For Rosie with love — G.M.

For my Richmond River cousins — S.M.K.

1. Red-Kite Kind of Wishes

Scarlet was the oldest of the Silk sisters. Tishkin was the youngest, but she died in the night while the others were sleeping, without a kiss or a cry or one last goodbye. The Rainbow Girls, Scarlet, Indigo, Violet, Amber and Saffron, and their brother, Griffin, remembered how terrible it was to wake and find their smallest one gone, before she had words or walking or even a name.

The Kingdom of Silk was a place where wishes sometimes come true. But even there, you couldn't wish away something that had already happened, no matter how much you wanted to, or how tightly you closed your eyes, or how hard you clenched your fists when you wished. Nell said the best you can wish for is that it never happens again. Now she was fifteen, Scarlet wasn't certain whether wishes could ever come true. She had yet to discover what could be done with black tights and a broken bridge.

Nell grandmothered the Silks, told them true things she had learnt over her many years of living. She was old and wise, and perhaps a little magic, as many grandmothers are. Nell said Grandmother Magic is left over from childhood; that we are all born with magic in us but many of us forget about it when we are grown up. Nell was loved and listened to. And so all Nell's Silks, even Scarlet, wished no one else would leave their home the way Tishkin did – without a goodbye, and until forever. But when Griffin and Layla wished it, they wished a little more as well; the little more was: *until we are grown up enough not to be sad.*

Wishes like that are deep and silent and don't need to be said. Made-aloud wishes are usually for fun and not important at all. For example, you might wish, like Griffin and Layla, that the rules were changed so dessert is always eaten before the main course, or you got your name printed in *The Guinness Book of Records* for collecting the most caterpillars from the cabbage patch, or you owned a red kite that would fly and never fall. It didn't matter much to Griffin and Layla whether these things came true or not.

Their pleasure came from sharing red-kite kind of wishes.

And that is exactly what they were doing one hot Tuesday in December. The teachers of Saint Benedict's were having a conference about next year's curriculum and students were not required to attend school. Layla never forgot to give her mother *not-required-to-attend* notes. And she quickly followed the giving of them by suggesting she stay at Griffin's house for the day, reminding Mrs Elliott there was always someone at home at the Kingdom of Silk. Always.

So that is why Griffin and Layla were inside the feed shed on that hot December morning, building a 'little-pig, little-pig, let-me-come-in' kind of house, with yellow straw bales and a hessian-sack roof. Their house of straw smelt sweet and summery inside, and Griffin and Layla nestled like birdlets in the loose scattered hay, picking grass seeds from their peeled-off socks and making Christmas wishes.

First they wished wishes for themselves. Griffin wished for a complete set of encyclopaedias bound in blue, with golden titles on their spines. A set exactly the right size to fill the gap on the top shelf of his bookcase, between *Gargoyles and Griffins in Architecture* and *The Comprehensive Illustrated Ornithologist's Bible*. Then he wished Layla could spend Christmas at the Kingdom of Silk. And, last, he wished for boots in a box. Layla's eyebrows shot up at this wish, because Griffin was a barefoot kind of boy. But it wasn't boots Griffin wanted at all.

'Then I would give the boots to Nell,' he said, 'and keep the box to put my crickets in.' Griffin had a whole family of crickets. They shared a Black Magic chocolate box with his collection of foil wrappers and sang to him at night.

Layla wished for a baby brother. She had wanted one for as long as she could remember. Next, she wished she could celebrate Christmas at the Kingdom of Silk. Then she wished for a real and true piebald pony and a pair of elbow-length pink satin gloves, exactly like the ones she'd seen in the window of the charity shop.

After that, Layla and Griffin wished a wish for each other and then one for everyone else, which altogether took a very long time. Then, because

everything inside the small straw house was good and golden, and there was no hairy-chinned wolf huffing and puffing outside, Griffin and Layla could think of nothing more to wish for.

In the hush that followed their red-kite wishing, Griffin began thinking about the deep and silent wish, and the little more as well, that only he and Layla had wished. He thought for as long as it took a mouse to steal an ear of wheat from a feed bin and drag it down a knothole in the floorboards.

Then Griffin said, 'I don't think we can wish a wish like that.'

'Why not?' asked Layla. She knew which wish Griffin meant because she had been thinking about it too. This is often the way of things when you are lying on your back in the hush and the hay with your best friend in the entire universe.

'It's the part about being grown up enough not to be sad. I don't think it can come true.'

'Why not?'

'Because when Tishkin died, Daddy and Mama cried as much as the rest of us. And they were grown up when it happened,' Griffin explained. 'And Nell's the oldest person I know and sometimes when she's talking about Tishkin, I can tell she's trying not to cry because her chin gets out of control.'

'Why don't we change the wish so it *can* come true?' said Layla.

'How?'

'Simple. We just make a wish that if anyone has to leave the Kingdom of Silk it won't be forever.'

'Can you wish things like that?'

'Why not?' said Layla. 'It's a good wish. It means that even if someone does have to go away, they'll always come back.'

So because it was almost Christmas, when wishes sometimes come true, and because he couldn't think of a better idea, Griffin agreed to change their wish.

Layla decided to write down the new wish to make it official. She'd brought her school journal with her because she'd persuaded her mother to let her sleep at the Silk's house and to catch the bus to school the next morning with Griffin and Perry Angel. Perry Angel was her second-best friend in the entire universe and the next-best thing to having a little brother of her very own.

8

When Layla had finished writing, Griffin said, 'Now I'll tell you what to put in the fine print.'

'What do you mean, "the fine print"?' asked Layla.

'It's the tiny writing at the end that people always forget to read until it's too late,' said Griffin. 'It tells you extra information. Just write this down: *This includes Perry Angel. Annie is his mama now because his other mother left him at the Maxwell Street Welfare Office when she was sweet sixteen and couldn't look after him properly.*'

Layla kept forgetting what came next and sometimes Griffin had to help her spell the words. But at last she said, 'Finished!'

'There's more,' said Griffin.

'Oh Griff, my hand's nearly worn out!'

'It's important,' said Griffin firmly and Layla sighed.

'What is it then?' she asked with a hint of grumpiness in her voice.

'*It also means Layla Elliott*,' said Griffin.

Layla looked up from her journal. 'You mean *that's* what you want me to write?'

Griffin nodded and Layla beamed.

'And after you've finished, write: *because Griffin's daddy said Layla was sent to comfort them after Tishkin went away. Also because Layla's mother said she might as well have been born a Silk on account of how much time she spends at their place.*'

When Layla had finished the fine print, she and Griffin read through the wish together.

'That's better,' said Griffin.

'What about Blue?' asked Layla.

'He's family.'

'I know, but he's different to the rest of us, so maybe the wish won't work if we don't write him in the fine print.'

'Okay,' said Griffin, 'let's put him in just in case.'

Without any help from Griffin, Layla wrote: *And Blue because he is part of the Silk family except he is really a dog and not a person. Blue is deaf but we think he can lip-read. He might feel sad if he knew he wasn't exactly like us. So we don't mention it, because dogs have feelings too.*

She peeled off a smiley-face sticker she'd been given for doing five journal entries in a row without any crossing out, and stuck it next to the fine print section, so people wouldn't forget to read it. Then she and Griffin crawled out through the doorway of their straw house and set off to find Perry and Nell.

2. To-ings, Fro-ings and the Four Strong Winds

Perry and Nell were not wishing for anything. They were outside having lessons. Nell was relaxing in her deckchair on the raft wearing a large, black, three-cornered hat. Zeus, her one-eyed pet crow, was perched on the mast. Blue lay on the very edge of the raft with a patch over one eye and his nose between his paws. He was supervising Perry, who was doing the doggie paddle in the dam wearing red armbands, green goggles and a large and extremely realistic fake tattoo of an anchor on his left shoulder.

When Layla and Griffin arrived at the dam, they realised at once Nell had used her Grandmother Magic to transform the Kingdom of Silk. It was now a place where galleons laden with treasure sailed the seven seas and pirates carried wicked-looking cutlasses clamped between their teeth. But even pirates have to go to school and what better place to learn than Nasty Nellie's Floating Academy for Pirates and Plunderers?

It was because of Miss Cherry, from Saint Benedict's School, that Perry had pirate lessons. It was she who had first noticed Perry's different way of learning. Miss Cherry knew that children with a different way of learning needed teachers with a different way of teaching. She also knew that Nell and Annie Silk were experts in different ways of teaching. And so, on Tuesdays and on Thursdays, Perry Angel had lessons at home with Nell or with Annie and sometimes with them both.

Nell and Annie didn't take any days off for conferences because they could speak to each other about the curriculum whenever they felt like it. They could also change the timetable at short notice. For instance, on a misty, mushroomy morning Nell might say to Perry, 'Let's have Nature Study this morning instead of Arithmetic.'

Then she and Perry would put on their yellow raincoats and black gumboots and splash through the puddles to Mr Canning's orchard to look for fairy rings in the rain-spangled grass. Or if a storm threatened while they were watching the robin redbreast build her nest in the Cox's Orange Pippin, Nell might schedule a cookery lesson instead.

Perry liked cooking classes but was not so keen on history. When Nell discovered this, she introduced a new topic called The History of Classic Australian Cuisine and included some excellent lessons including: *How a Singer Named Melba Turned into a Pudding*, *Why Ballerinas Prefer Pavlova Without Strawberries on Top* and *Lord Lamington's Contribution to Australian Cooking*.

Nell always began these lessons with the words,

Once upon a time, and usually ended them with a cooking demonstration. Soon Perry began to look forward to Nell's historical cooking classes. As well as finding out about some very interesting people who lived in the olden days, Perry learned to cook and count, to measure and mix, sift and stir and sprinkle.

On in-between days Perry had lessons in Miss Cherry's classroom. He liked Miss Cherry, who had cheeks like her name. He also liked his grown-up friend and classroom helper, Mr Jenkins, and Mr Davis, the bus driver who called him Buddy. So as much as Perry loved learning with his grandmother and his mother, he didn't mind going to school.

Layla and Griffin went to Saint Benedict's every day except weekends but would much rather have gone to Nasty Nellie's Academy. They had been there before and knew the ropes. *Knowing the ropes* is pirate language for *knowing how things work*.

Everyone had their own piratey name, including the raft. She was christened *Sweet Suzy* with a bottle of Nell's homemade ginger beer tipped over her bow. Nell was Nasty Nellie the Pirate Queen. Layla was Sinbad the Sailor, Griffin was Jack Tar and Perry was Davey Jones. Even Blue played along. He was Long John Silver and Zeus was Jolly Roger, keeping a lookout from the mast and squawking a warning when he saw an enemy on the horizon. If Ben joined in, he was Barnacle Ben and when Annie came, she was Lorelei, the beautiful maiden who tried to lure the pirate ship onto the rocks with her songs.

When she saw Griffin and Layla, Nasty Nellie raised a cling film tube telescope to her eye. 'Shiver me timbers, there be trouble on the horizon! Ahoy there. State your business, land lubbers!'

Sinbad giggled, then cupped her hands around her mouth. 'We want to board, Captain.' For the moment she forgot all about the wish and stripped down to the swimming costume she wore under her clothes.

'Surrender your weapons, you scoundrels!' shouted the Pirate Queen.

'We haven't got any weapons, Nasty Nellie,' said Jack Tar, peeling off his T-shirt.

'No weapons! What sort of pirate has no weapons? Come aboard this instant and I'll find you some swords,' said Nasty Nellie.

Sinbad tossed her journal on the pile of discarded clothes. Then she and Jack Tar raced into the water and swam to *Sweet Suzy*. As they hauled themselves on board, the pirate vessel bobbed and dipped dangerously low in the water. But the Pirate Queen was perfectly safe, because Barnacle Ben was a carpenter in his spare time and had nailed the legs of her chair to the deck in case of stormy seas.

'Welcome to the Academy,' said Nasty Nellie, clutching the armrests of her seat until *Sweet Suzy* steadied. Then she picked up a black pillowcase decorated with a white skull and crossbones and emptied out its contents. There were two enormous black felt moustaches, an assortment of eye patches, a pair of large golden hoop earrings, several spotted scarves and a stuffed shoulder-parrot. Last of all, two magnificent plywood cutlasses with plastic jewels stuck on the handles and wickedly curved gold-painted blades clattered onto the deck.

'If you want to join our classes, you'd better make yourselves look respectable with some of these. You've already missed out on adding-ups and taking-aways,' said the Pirate Queen, filling her hand with copper coins and letting them trickle through her fingers back into the bucket beside her. 'Most important for pirates to know their adding-ups for when they find treasure, and their taking-aways for when other pirates steal it.'

Then she pointed to Davey Jones with a pair of barbecue tongs sticking out from the end of her sleeve, the result of a terrible battle she'd fought with a shark.

'Jones be learning to stay afloat in rough weather now, and growing strong muscles for digging holes and burying treasures. You can join him if you like.'

Jack Tar lowered himself carefully off the edge of *Sweet Suzy* so as not to dislodge his moustache. But Sinbad forgot about hers and did a belly-whacker that sent up a water spout higher than a blue whale's. The sea grew choppy and Long John Silver jumped in next to Davey Jones and doggie paddled beside him for encouragement.

After a while the Pirate Queen leaned down from her deckchair. With her one good hand and the barbecue tongs, she pulled a rope attached to *Sweet Suzy* at one end and looped around Davey Jones's middle at the other. Then she hauled him towards the raft, like a net of sardines.

'Your lips be as blue as the briny, Jones,' she said.

Pirates usually call the sea 'the briny' and people by their last name and get their 'bes' and their 'ares' mixed up, like this: 'Be you cold?'

Davey Jones clung to the edge of the raft, shivering so much he could barely speak. But as brave as could be and in proper pirate talk he said, 'Nnnnnnno, I be nnnnnnot ccccccold.'

Nasty Nellie was not convinced. She put the cardboard telescope to her eye and did an up-close inspection of Jones's lips. 'You'd better come aboard and dry off, me hearty.'

Sinbad and Jack Tar helped Jones and his mate, Long John Silver, scramble aboard. They untied the rope from around Jones's middle because his fingers wouldn't work properly and the Pirate Queen towelled his hair dry and then the rest of him.

'Nnnnnnot that bbbit,' he said, pointing to the very realistic fake tattoo on his shoulder. Then, because even pirate grandmothers have a soft spot in their hearts, especially for small, blue-lipped pirates with fake tattoos, the Pirate Queen cuddled Davey Jones on her lap.

When his bones at last stopped rattling she said, 'Gather round crew, while we study the charts and plot a course to our next destination.' She rummaged around in her piratey pillowcase, pulled out something which looked like a large deflated beach ball and handed it to Jack Tar. 'Blow a stiff southerly into that for me, Tar.'

Jack Tar blew till he was giddy and green and the ball had expanded into a globe of indigo and amethyst, crimson, emerald and sunflower yellow. A plastic world of sapphire seas, dusty deserts and juicy jungles, of archipelagos and isthmuses. A paradise for pirates.

Sweet Suzy and her captain and crew sailed by the Galapagos Islands, the Rock of Gibraltar and Arctic icebergs. They charted a course along latitudes, down longitudes, over the Tropic of Capricorn, under the Tropic of Cancer and across the exotic equator. They sailed north and south and east and west. And when they stepped ashore, they saw wonders such as lily pickers, fire eaters, chimney sweepers, and tigers' teeth and tails and toes.

But by lunchtime, the Pirate Queen and her crew decided that of all the islands, continents and countries, home was best and they set sail for the Kingdom of Silk, at Cameron's Creek, Australia.

'When are we doing the dancing and singing, Nasty Nellie?' Sinbad reminded the Pirate Queen.

'When Barnacle Ben returns from his voyage to the unknown.'

'I thought he was coming back early today,' said Jack Tar, shading his eyes with his hand, straining to see Barnacle Ben's Bedford sailing over the horizon.

'So he was, so he was. But a pirate's life be ruled by the to-ings and fro-ings of the tides and by the four strong winds. And not even the Queen of Pirates has power over them, me hearties. Now, weigh anchor, trim the sails and steer us through the heads.'

Jack Tar and Sinbad took an oar each. Dodging man-eating sharks and monstrous squid, they rowed to the rickety jetty and moored *Sweet Suzy* in the safe harbour of the Kingdom of Silk.

Once their feet touched land, Perry and Blue went to fetch Annie from her studio and Nell waited while Layla and Griffin dressed themselves. When Layla picked up her journal she remembered the rewritten wish and opened the page to show Nell.

'Look, Nell,' she said. 'Look what I wrote in my journal. Griff and me thought it up this morning.'

Nell read everything Layla had written, the large print and the fine. Here and there she smiled and at the end she sighed a little.

'It's a lovely wish,' she said, 'but you know none of us can stay forever, no matter how much we want to.'

Then, before anyone had time to feel too sad, she said in her best buccaneer's voice, 'Right, now I be going to the galley to sample a sardine or two. Who be coming with me?'

3. The Buccaneers' Banquet

When pirates speak of sardines, they don't mean the sort that come in cans with tiny keys to wind open their lids. They mean fresh ones with gills and scales and fins and tails.

For lunch, Perry, Griffin and Layla dusted the fish's silver skins with flour. Nell fried them quick and crunchy and golden, and served them with chunks of Annie's crusty bread, squeezings of

lemony oil, sprigs of dill, salad greens and sun-warmed cherry-cheeked tomatoes from her garden. There were tiny glass dishes, pinch-pots, piled high with flakes of soft white sea salt for scattering.

Perry Angel wondered if sardines grew up to be whales. He sometimes wished he could meet a whale. In dreams his wish came true. These dreams were always blue and filled with strangely beautiful music. Whale songs. In his dreams Perry could understand what the whales were singing about.

They were singing to their children, telling them which way to go and calling them home. Sometimes when Nell was talking to him, Perry thought she sounded like the whales in his dreams.

Layla shut her eyes while she was eating and thought she heard the sea, though it was more than a hundred kilometres away. When she told the others, Nell said, 'You see, that's why pirates have such good hearing, because they eat a lot of sardines.'

Perry wondered if Nell had been a pirate before she became a grandmother because she seemed to know so much about them.

For dessert there were rum balls. Rum is a nasty-tasting drink, which burns your throat and makes your legs wobbly. It is a pirate's next favourite thing after treasure and sardines. But, like the black moustaches Griffin and Layla had worn and the tattoo on Perry's arm, Auntie Ruby's Rum Balls were fakes. They didn't have even a splash of rum in them, on account of Nell's plan to sing sea shanties and dance the sailor's hornpipe when Ben got home.

'Too much rum makes pirates forget the words
and the tune and most other things as well,' she
explained, 'and sometimes they get so wobbly they
fall overboard.'

Auntie Ruby hadn't made the rum balls; Nell
had. Because Ruby was Nell's auntie and she died
when Nell was a young girl. It was only the recipe

and the bluebird plate the rum balls were on that were Auntie Ruby's. She'd written the recipe in pencil on the back of a used envelope, especially for Nell. The front of the envelope had a stamp with a picture of a queen on it. Not the Pirate Queen, the Queen of England, when she was very young. It was a blue stamp and it cost a shilling which is old money for ten cents. The apron Nell was wearing when she cooked the buccaneers' banquet also had a picture of the Queen of England on it. Nell had a lot of aprons, but this one was her favourite, even though Her Majesty was slightly faded.

'Long ago, before Her Majesty was born,' said Nell, wiping a dribble of sardine juice off the queen's nose, 'pirates sailed the seas of England.' Nell believed there were lessons to be learned in everything including buccaneers' banquets, royal aprons and hand-me-down recipes.

4. Cake Talk

Almost all the recipes pasted into Nell's spiral-bound cookery book with flour-and-water glue were hand-me-downs. Most had been handwritten by the people who had given them to Nell. Often the writing was faded and the paper yellowed. Nell thought of these recipes as pieces of other people's lives, given away like slices of Armenian Love Cake with a cup of tea. Or rag patches on a quilt from wedding gowns or naming-day layettes with buttons and bows from birthday frocks. Tiny treasures to keep forever. Nell knew most of them by heart, but she sometimes read her recipe book the way other people might read a novel. Sometimes she laughed as she read. Sometimes she cried.

Of all the Silks, it was Amber who loved Nell's recipe book best and Nell had promised it would be hers some day. Amber had already started her own collection of recipes.

Amber came right in the middle of the Rainbow Girls. Scarlet was special because she came first. Next came Indigo and Violet. Just being twins made them special. Saffron was special now Tishkin was gone, because she was the youngest of Ben and Annie Silk's five daughters. Griffin's specialness came from being a boy, the only boy in the family until Perry Angel arrived. But Perry hadn't come from the quiet dark inside Annie, like all the others. He came on the ten-thirty express. So Griffin stayed special and Perry was special too, each in his very own way. And baby Tishkin, who was born before the daisies bloomed and left without a goodbye, still held a special place in everyone's heart.

Amongst all this specialness, Amber might have felt ordinary. True, she was the only one in the family whose hair grew in copper coils as tiny and tight as the springs inside ballpoint pens. And not one of the other Rainbow Girls had fairy dust on her nose. But although these things made Amber different she sometimes wondered if they made her special.

Nell could have told Amber it doesn't matter where you come in the family or what you look like, it's the things you do and say and what you are like on the inside that matters. But Amber didn't ask Nell or anyone else. Instead she cooked, because a cake could say all the things she couldn't.

Amber discovered this when Elsie's Bert died. Elsie was Mrs Rasmussen who looked after the post office and Herbert was her husband. He was tall and thin and was called Bert for short. He went fishing in the creek a lot while Elsie stayed in the post office. She sold balls of parcel string and books

of stamps and took your money for the electricity bill and put your letters in a tiny black box with a door and a silver key if you didn't have a proper letterbox.

Elsie's heart was broken when her Bert died. She and Amber had known each other from when Amber was small enough to fit on the parcel scales. But even so, Amber couldn't tell Elsie how sad she felt about Bert. Instead she made an Armenian Love Cake in a heart-shaped pan. She put it in her bicycle basket in Nell's white cake tin with the blue lid and cornflowers painted on the front and rode to the post office. It was past closing time, so Amber walked around the back to where Elsie lived. When Elsie opened the door Amber took the lid off the tin so she could see the cake. Then the crickets sang on the soft green banks of the creek at the bottom of the garden. Elsie and Amber said nothing to each other and quietly remembered Bert-for-short in his striped braces and his tartan cap with his bamboo fishing pole and homemade feather flies and his loud, scratchy breathing.

At last Elsie said, 'Did you make it?'

Amber nodded.

'Thank you, Amber, it's a lovely sorry cake,'
Elsie said.

After Elsie's cake, Amber began to make sorry

cakes, thank-you cakes, cheer-up cakes, goodbye cakes, get-well cakes, welcome cakes and I-love-you cakes. It seemed almost magical that the person receiving the cake knew exactly what Amber wanted to say. It was cake language. But sometimes Amber made *just-because* cakes. She made them for fun because people couldn't work out what they meant, no matter how good they were at cake language.

Even when Amber wasn't cooking she was thinking about cooking.

On that warm and wishful afternoon when the captain and crew of *Sweet Suzy* feasted on finny, scaly, gilly, taily, salty sea sardines, Amber was over the hills and far away at high school with her Rainbow sisters. Her maths teacher filled the blackboard with adding-ups and taking-aways and her classmates copied sums and wrote answers into their exercise books. But Amber wrote a list of ingredients, because Nell had promised that on Saturday they would start their Christmas cooking.

5. The Plum-Pudding Planetarium

On Friday morning before school Layla packed her pyjamas and toothbrush and her Wish Pony with the removable saddle and brushable tail into her pink backpack. She planned to walk home with Griffin after school and spend the night at the Kingdom of Silk so she could help with the Christmas cooking from the very beginning. Mrs Elliott walked to the gate with Layla and passed her a plastic shopping bag.

'Give those to Nell Silk,' she said, 'and tell her
they're for making stars.'

Six months before, Layla had told her mother
that Nell wanted to make stars for Christmas
decorations.

'Nell says it's a shame milk bottles don't have foil
lids on them anymore.'

'Tell Mrs Silk tart tins might do,' said Mrs
Elliott.

'But Nell makes the old-fashioned kind of tarts you cook in metal tins,' said Layla.

'I should have known,' said Mrs Elliott in a very quiet voice with no ups and downs in it.

'Yes you should have, Mum,' Layla said, 'Nell's an old-fashioned kind of lady. She's a bit like our nana was, only magic.'

Mrs Elliott sighed and began to think of Layla's nana and of other old-fashioned things. She remembered sitting on the floor with her mother and sisters, surrounded by mountains of shiny milk bottle lids, some silver, others red, green or blue, their mother poking holes with a knitting needle and passing the caps to her girls, Louisa, Katrina and Caroline. She and her sisters threaded the lids onto lengths of wool. Mrs Elliott remembered the scent of a real Christmas tree, of wishing for a piebald pony, and of still feeling happy when she got a homemade rag doll and a book instead.

The Saturday after she had remembered all these things, Mrs Caroline Elliott did something surprising. She went to the bakery and bought six jam tarts: three raspberry and three lemon. The next week she did the same, and the week after, and the week after. Mrs Elliott bought six jam tarts every Saturday for six months even though she didn't care for the taste of jam tarts at all.

On that Friday morning in December, when Layla looked into the plastic shopping bag, her eyes shone as brightly as the dozens of empty jam tart tins she saw there. She flung her arms around her mother's neck and kissed her. Mrs Elliott waved Layla goodbye and because it was the season of wishfulness, she wished for a moment that she was going to the Kingdom of Silk with her daughter that afternoon, to sit on the floor and make stars.

It was really Scarlet's turn to make breakfast that Saturday, but she had a part-time job at Mr Kadri's Colour Patch Café and had to start early. So Nell made pancakes and served them warm with poached apricots, cinnamon, brown sugar and vanilla yoghurt.

Tart-tin stars were not the only stars made in Nell's kitchen that day. There were buttery shortbread ones too, sprinkled with vanilla sugar. Amber weighed and mixed the ingredients, Griffin rolled the dough, Perry cut it with a star-shaped cutter, Layla sprinkled the stars with sugar and Annie put them in the oven to cook.

While the golden shortbreads cooled on wire racks, it was time to start making the plum puddings. Twelve squares of cloth were spread out on the bench to wrap twelve Christmas puddings.

'Why do you make so many, Nell?' asked Layla.

'I make enough to go around, some for seconds, some for afters and the rest for leftovers,' said Nell, measuring the raisins, sultanas, currants, figs and plums and fat red cherries.

'What Nell really means is she makes leftovers on purpose,' said Annie, laughing.

'Who gets them all?' asked Layla.

'Well there's Mr Jenkins,' said Nell.

'Mr Jenkins gets a small one all to himself,' said Annie.

'He loves plum pudding,' said Nell. 'It reminds him of his Mrs Jenkins. She used to make them for him when she was alive.'

'And the Meals-on-Wheels ladies, Nell,' Annie said, but Nell was still thinking about Mr Jenkins all alone on Christmas Day frying slices of pudding in brandy and butter and missing his Juliette.

'They deliver pieces of Nell's pudding to the senior citizens of Cameron's Creek,' explained Annie. 'And then there's Melody. You remember Melody, don't you Layla?'

Layla nodded. Melody was the social worker who brought Perry to the Kingdom of Silk.

'Nell sends a plum-pudding package to Melody in the post. I think she shares it with children who don't have families to stay with at Christmas time, doesn't she, Nell?'

But Nell didn't hear a word. After she'd finished thinking about Mr Jenkins, she thought about Perry Angel's other mother who lived in a city by the sea, far away from Cameron's Creek. She wondered if Sunday Lee would have pudding on Christmas Day and someone to share it with. Then her thoughts went to Elsie-from-the-post-office and to Miss Cherry and her small scruffy dog. Nell's heart was gently squeezed and she wished everyone was as lucky as she was and could eat pudding with people they loved.

Christmas cooking is fun, but it is also hard work, so Perry Angel made a cubby house with tea-towel walls and a table roof. He crawled inside and lay on the rag rug with Blue, thinking about leftovers. On his seven-year journey to find the Kingdom of Silk, Perry had never met anyone who liked leftovers. Leftovers were things like cold peas, grey potatoes, stale bread and baby boys left on the steps of Welfare Offices. Nobody wanted them. But then Perry met Nell, and Nell said the world was a better place because of leftovers.

Above him, Amber added eggs, breadcrumbs, sugar, spices and flour to the mountain of moist fruit. Annie, Indigo and Violet wrapped the cooled shortbreads in cellophane parcels tied with red ribbon and sang a song about a baby and a drummer boy. Nell waterproofed the cloths with flour and water and filled them with pudding mixture. Then she lowered them carefully into boiling water in pots the size of witches' cauldrons and clouds of steam billowed into the rafters.

'Look!' said Saffron. 'It's dragon's breath!' And the children turned their sticky faces upwards. Even Perry crawled out to have a look.

After the puddings came Florentines: biscuits made of chopped cherries, honey, butter, cream and almond splinters, so thin you could almost see through them, like the stained-glass windows in Saint Benedict's Church. While the children measured, melted and mixed, and licked wooden spoons, the Christmas dragon hid in one of the cauldrons and breathed his cinnamon-scented breath into the heavenlies.

Then Ben came into the kitchen.

'Anyone ready for lunch?'

Ben had made pizza in his mud-brick oven near the dam. The Cox's Orange Pippin shaded the table set with jugs of icy homemade cordial, baskets of biscuits which weren't quite the right shape and platters of pizza slices.

After they had eaten, the children lay down,

dreamy and drowsy, in the lap of the earth with beetles, bugs and butterflies. Nell leaned her back against the tree trunk and closed her eyes. But Saffron, who had been thinking about the dragon in the kitchen, said, 'Tell us about magic, Nell. Please.'

And Nell agreed, because magic was one of her favourite topics.

'We're all born with magic in us,' she said. 'A child's magic is so powerful it sometimes rubs off on grown-up people. When that happens, they re-discover their own leftover magic and all kinds of remarkable things happen. Their limpy legs grow stronger and they don't need as many naps. The words of long-forgotten songs and stories come back into their heads. Sometimes they compose completely new tunes and whistle them on red buses in the mornings when they're going to the library to borrow books about interesting topics like magic puddings or very hungry caterpillars. And on cold, dark, dismal days they see fire-breathing dragons and knights in shining armour, where once they saw only clouds. People like this laugh loudly and often, and they smile more, because they've discovered the marvellous secret that leftover magic is a cure for gloominess and loneliness and...'

'Boringness?' asked Layla.

But Nell had put herself to sleep. So Violet and Indigo went inside and came back with old magazines, scraps of wallpaper, paint, scissors and glue. Layla fetched her bag of jam-tart tins and while Nell slept, the children made Chinese lanterns, tart-tin stars and a paper chain that was longer than forever. Then they climbed into the tree house and wrapped the chain around the appled boughs and tied stars and lanterns among the leaves with tinsel threads. They cheered when it was done, and Nell woke up and said it was the best Christmas tree she'd ever seen.

Ben carried a ladder inside and the children followed and passed him the rest of the stars to hang from the ceiling of the passageway. Nell suggested they call them the Caroline Elliott galaxy.

All that was left to do that evening was to tie the cooked, cloth-wrapped puddings from the rafters. There was Mercury, Venus, Earth, Mars,

Jupiter, Saturn, Uranus and Neptune and even tiny Pluto although, as Nell explained, it wasn't strictly a planet.

'What are the other three?' asked Layla.

'They're undiscovered planets,' said Nell.

By the time Scarlet came home, Nell's kitchen had been transformed into a plum-pudding planetarium.

6. Hot Yellow Peaches and Holes in the Sky

When Scarlet first started her Saturday job at the Colour Patch Café, she had to wash dishes. Amber thought it was odd that Scarlet got a job washing dishes when she tried to get out of doing them at home whenever she could. But then Anik came and Scarlet got a promotion. Mr Kadri taught her how to make raspberry spiders and banana splits and clear the tables while Anik washed the dishes.

Anik was fifteen and lived with his grandmother,
two aunties and his uncle above Mr Kadri's Colour
Patch Café. Anik walked gracefully, watchfully, like
the herons that waded between ribbons of sunlight
in the shallows of Cameron's Creek. Anik took his
first steps in a faraway land where children walked
as lightly as shadows, as cautiously as cats, for fear
of disturbing buried bombs.

Mr Kadri had once lived in a village like Anik's.
He had once wondered if he would ever see his
family again. He knew how it felt to be a painter
of pictures, putting pig meat in plastic bags, hosing
blood off concrete floors. He understood what
it was like to be surrounded by words he didn't
understand and faces he didn't know.

Because of all these things, Mr Kadri wanted Anik and his family to have someone to come home to at night. Someone who understood how they felt and who would try to fill the empty places in their lives.

So that is why the Kadris shared their small upstairs home with Anik and his family. That is why they paid for Anik's Advanced English lessons and why Anik so willingly washed mountains of dishes in the kitchen of the Colour Patch Café. It is why Mrs Kadri cooked for them while Anik's grandma bounced the babies on her knees and sang them lullabies. And because every child is born filled with magic, the Kadri's curly haired babies understood Anik's granny's songs before they had words of their own. They laughed and smiled and sucked and slept and Anik's grandma closed her eyes and imagined she was young again. She dreamt the babies she sang to were her own and that wishes sometimes came true.

Scarlet shared a seat with Anik on the bus that took them to school. She wanted to know things about Anik. Small things like the sound of his laughter, middle-sized things like his favourite poem and big things like where his mother and father were. But the bus was filled with the sound of other people's conversations. Their words were quick and loud and strange to Anik's ears. And his English words seemed slow and clumsy. So he kept them mostly to himself. In the afternoons Anik went to Advanced English lessons and afterwards passed the words he had learnt on to his grandmother and aunties and uncle. And in the evenings, when the Colour Patch Café was closed and its neon sign stained the street with all the colours of paradise, Anik and Mr Kadri and their families squeezed around the old green laminex table in the kitchen and shared words and signs, laughter and food and friendship.

Scarlet wanted to share these things with Anik, too. So when she worked at the Colour Patch Café she took tray-loads of used sundae dishes, coffee cups, soup bowls, silver teapots and spider glasses for Anik to wash and words for him to listen to. And each week when she came he talked more often and sometimes laughed.

On the Saturday when everyone at the Kingdom of Silk was doing their Christmas cooking and while Scarlet filled salt cellars, sauce bottles and pepper mills, she asked Anik about before.

Anik's arms stayed deep and still in the washing-up water and his eyes stared blindly at the bubbles. For as long as it took Scarlet to fill all the salt cellars, Anik stayed silent. Then he said, 'My father is a fisherman. My mother weaves baskets. I have two small sisters. Our country is at war for many years. But we are fishers and weavers and children. We are not soldiers. We have no weapons. Then one day I go to school and when I come home...'

Anik paused and Scarlet wished she could turn back time and ask only the small things. She was afraid of what Anik might say. But she said nothing to stop him and Anik went on.

'When I return there is no home. There is only smoke and fire and soldiers. My village is burning. My house is gone. I hear guns and I run very fast.

I run two days and then I am at my grandmother's house.'

Anik's words spilled out like hot soup. Scarlet passed him a paper napkin to sop his tears. She didn't know what else to do, what to say. She couldn't imagine coming home to nothing, no one. Her only comforting thought was that there had been a grandmother for Anik to run to.

All the way to the Kingdom of Silk, Scarlet thought about Anik and his family and about other fishermen and basketmakers and children who have never lived in peace.

It was dusk when Scarlet reached home. The sun was a hot yellow peach in a sea of strawberry sauce and the moon was a paper doily tossed up high. When she was very small Scarlet thought the moon was a hole in the sky and if she could only get up there and go through, she'd find another shiny universe inside it. The rusty gate squealed shut behind her and she trudged up the long gravel driveway, closer to the yellow lights of home, closer to the moon.

Delicious aromas wafted from the open windows: cinnamon and nutmeg, oranges and cloves. From the veranda Scarlet looked through the screen door and saw the galaxy of twinkling tart-tin stars turning slowly on tinsel threads. She heard the sound of a soup-pot snare drum and singing. To Scarlet's left the kitchen door was open. She saw her daddy standing on a ladder and Mama handing him fat cloth-wrapped puddings to hang from the rafters.

No one heard Scarlet arrive. No one saw her standing at the door in the dusky light, caught between two places. She had reached her hole in the sky, the safe and shiny universe of the Kingdom of Silk where the only danger was imaginary pirates. Children ran carelessly fast here and laughed out loud and danced the Spanish Fandango and wishes sometimes came true. Scarlet wondered if children on the other side of the world ever looked at the moon and imagined a better place. A place like hers.

There is a poem painted on the door of the house at the Kingdom of Silk. It's Nell's favourite because it helps her stay calm in the storms of life. Annie painted it for her when Ben first brought them there to live. Scarlet had read the poem many times before that night, but hadn't thought much about its meaning. There were other poems she liked better.

But on Saturday night, Scarlet wanted to feel calm, so she read Nell's poem again. It seemed to be about opposites. Things like crying and laughing, finding and losing, loving and hating. Scarlet knew very well about all these things, but when she reached the words, *A time for war and a time for peace* she wondered, 'Did this mean forever? Would there always be wars?'

Scarlet turned her back on the moon and marched into the kitchen. She slammed her bag and her black apron on the table and shouted, 'That's a stupid poem. I hate it!'

Then she stormed down the hallway to the bedroom she shared with Amber, leaving the Caroline Elliott galaxy shivering in her wake.

7. Unsayable Things and Eiderdowns

Later, when Nell was resting amongst the feathery hills and downy valleys of her eiderdown, Scarlet crept into her bedroom and slid between the sheets. Nell's arms went around her the way they had so many times before. Scarlet stared out the window where stars pricked holes in the darkness like tiny promises of brighter tomorrows and she wondered how to explain the things she felt inside. Frightening things like, *I don't know if I believe in making wishes anymore* and *why doesn't someone stop bad things happening?*

But many unsayable things have been said because of eiderdowns and a grandmother's arms.

'I'm so sorry I was mean tonight, Nell,' whispered Scarlet. 'I don't really hate your poem. I just don't want it to be true.'

'You're forgiven for shouting,' said Nell, 'but you don't have to apologise for disagreeing with someone or something. What don't you like about the poem?'

'Will there always be wars?' Scarlet asked, hoping for an answer like a star. But not even grandmothers are wise enough to know everything.

'I hope not,' said Nell, 'but I thought people would have seen enough of them by now to realise there must be a better way.'

'You once told us we can't wish away something that's already happened, but we can wish it never happens again,' said Scarlet. 'That doesn't work with war does it? Wishing's not enough.'

Then Scarlet cried. She cried for Anik and for his mother and father and two sisters who might

never see one another again. She cried for Anik's two aunties, his uncle and his grandmother who had seen and heard things they could not speak of. She cried for all the other children and aunties and uncles and grandmothers who still lived in places where there were wars. And she cried because she was afraid wishes didn't really come true at all. Not for Anik's people, and not even for people like her.

When Scarlet's tears had stopped, Nell said, 'I can't tell you how to fix something as big as this, Scarlet. All I know is you're not the only one who wants an end to war. Even in small towns like Cameron's Creek, there are other people who have exactly the same wish as you. So imagine how many of us there must be on the planet. Maybe if we all did something small we could make a difference. Who knows, we might even change the way other people think.'

Scarlet went back to her own bed, wondering what small step she could take in the morning to start changing the world.

8. Kiss-Me-Quick and Kryptonite

The following morning Scarlet lay on the old red couch by the veranda steps. One foot was propped on the armrest with her freshly painted toenails drying in the breeze. She had a pure white quill from Ginger the goose, a bottle of red food colouring and a pad of clean white paper on her lap. A pair of Nell's old spectacles with rhinestone-studded purple frames was perched on the end

of her nose. Scarlet was wearing them to try to understand the world wisely, the way Nell did. She dipped her quill in the dye and wrote a red poem for Anik on the soft white skin on the inside of her arm while she wondered what she could do to change the world.

Indigo, Violet and Layla were swimming in the dam. Nell and Annie were being lifesavers. Amber was making lavender and lemonade scones for morning tea. Ben was in his shed. Annie said he was doing secret men's business. But he wasn't really. He was just sitting, looking at a pile of old timber which used to be a bridge and wondering what he could make from it.

Griffin had camouflaged himself with mud and was stalking lizards in the pumpkin patch. He had decided to become a vegetarian and thought Zeus should be as well. His Sunday mission was relocating lizards to the wood pile where Zeus couldn't find them.

And Perry was doing his favourite thing, being Superman. He was wearing the costume Nell had made for him, all except his gumboots. He couldn't wear them because an echidna had crawled into one of them and was too prickly to be pulled out. On Sundays, Superman collected the eggs. He was brave and could do it by himself. He did everything exactly the way he'd seen Nell do it.

Blue guarded the gate while Superman went inside and scattered a handful of golden grain over the ground. While the hens were eating, Superman said good morning to Madonna. Then he chatted to the others for a while about things like the weather and the size of the pumpkins growing in the vegetable patch and the Christmas puddings and the galaxy of tart-tin stars. He had to wait while one of the hens laid her egg. She clucked excitedly when she'd finished and Superman wondered if she had the same sort of feeling he got when he saved the entire universe from destruction. The hen jumped down from her nest and Superman picked up her warm egg and held it to his cheek before he put it in the old bent saucepan with the others. He thanked the chickens, because Nell said everyone likes to be appreciated for what they do. When he got close to the gate, Superman felt like flying a loop-the-loop and landing on top of Ben's shed with his cape flying out behind him because he'd done everything right.

On the way up to the house Superman counted the eggs, starting with the speckled one Madonna

had laid. But the others looked so much alike it was hard to remember which was which and he forgot where he was up to and had to start again.

When he got to the veranda steps, he saw Scarlet. Scarlet was scary. She was like Kryptonite. She made Superman lose all his powers and become Perry Angel again.

Perry had found something in common with almost everyone who lived at the Kingdom of Silk. Even Blue. Blue loved sprawling across Nell's knees and having his back scratched. So did Perry. Amber liked cooking and so did Perry. Ben liked sitting in the shed, whistling and whittling soft green willow sticks and so did Perry. Then there was singing with Annie, painting pictures of deep mystery like Indigo and wearing wings like Layla.

Perry and Griffin often crossed the paddocks together and climbed the daisied hills where they lay on their stomachs sharing Ben's binoculars and watching hawks hover in the never-ending sky.

And Perry spent hours with Violet, picking posies of pansies, Sweet Alice, Johnny-jump-ups, jonquils and japonica. He made bouquets of baby's breath, kiss-me-quick, love-in-a-mist, granny's bonnets and forget-me-nots and learnt their pretty names. He and Violet pressed their petals flat between the leaves of large heavy books. And weeks later they peeked between the pages to see the everlasting flowers they had made, flowers for keeping, for remembering and for putting in homemade paper.

There was nothing at all that Perry didn't like doing with Nell. They looked for fairies amongst the bees when Nell was inspecting the hive. They walked in the rain, chatted to chickens, played pirates, danced the Spanish Fandango and ten million other things as well.

The only person Perry seemed to share nothing with was Scarlet. So it surprised him when she waved a leg at him this Sunday morning and said, 'Want to do my other foot, Superman?'

Scarlet had never called Perry Superman before and today he wasn't even in full uniform. It seemed like a good sign. So Perry sat the saucepan of eggs carefully on the top step, took the small bottle of red enamel from Scarlet's outstretched hand and began to paint her toenails. It wasn't nearly as much fun as painting deep mysteries and because he was nervous, Perry kept accidentally going over the lines and getting the red on Scarlet's toes.

When Perry had finished, Scarlet screwed the cap back on the bottle and put her foot up next to the other one. Perry held his breath while she looked at her toes with her slanting sea-green eyes.

'Good job, Superman,' she said. 'Want to hear a poem?'

Superman wasn't sure. Sometimes poems are hard to understand, even for superheroes. But he wanted to please Scarlet, so he nodded his head and Scarlet patted the couch beside her.

'Come on, lie down next to me. There's plenty of room.' She slid closer to the buttoned back of the couch, put her arm around his shoulders and drew him down beside her. He rested his head on the fringed and faded cushion beside Scarlet's and tried to put his feet up on the other end next to hers. But they wouldn't reach. Blue leapt up in the space at the end of the couch, turned around

five times, scratched a lumpy cushion out of the way, then curled up with his chin on Superman's bare feet and sighed contentedly. Superman was Blue's favourite superhero. Blue didn't know it, but he had secret powers of his own. Whenever Superman was feeling frightened, nervous or worried, he had only to touch Blue and he started feeling braver.

Scarlet adjusted her sparkly spectacles. Superman's X-ray vision noticed there weren't any lenses in them, but he didn't mention it. Scarlet began to read.

'It's called "Being Scarlet",' she said.

> 'Scarlet Silk is
> a teenager
> organises others
> not herself
> is
> mostly loud
> sometimes lazy
> often angry
> always loved
> is

mean
is nice
is scared of mice
is sometimes good
and sometimes bad
sometimes happy
sometimes sad.
Scarlet Silk
writes poems in red
won't make her bed
gets in fights
wears black tights
is
tragic
full of magic
blows schoolboys kisses
hates washing dishes.
Scarlet Silk
is
a mystery
to everyone
including
herself.'

Superman thought Scarlet had finished, but she looked at him and then wrote something else.

'and Superman.'

She showed Superman what she'd written and told him what it said. Then she laughed. 'Did you like it?'

Superman nodded.

The poem sounded exactly like Scarlet. But Superman hadn't realised before that Scarlet was a mystery to other people as well as to him, even to herself.

'You mean it? Really?' Scarlet made her eyes the shape of sardines and looked hard at Superman's face to see if she could tell what he was thinking.

Superman nodded again. 'It's good,' he said. 'I really like it.'

Scarlet turned back to her poem and read it quietly to herself. She sighed. Being Scarlet Silk wasn't easy.

9. Peace Talk and Pinking Shears

Scarlet decided that if she was going to change the world, she needed a list. There was nothing unusual about that. Scarlet had always been a keen list maker.

Amber didn't mean to peek. It happened by accident when she was making her bed. Unlike Scarlet, Amber enjoyed bed making. Holding the quilt by its bottom corners, she'd toss it high into

the air where it billowed like a yacht sail for a few seconds, before floating gracefully down and falling neatly into place on the bed. It had taken Amber lots of practice to be able to do this. Some days she did it twice. Other days she made Scarlet's bed, just for the fun of it.

That was how Amber saw Scarlet's list. On Monday morning before they went to school Amber made her own bed, then she sailed Scarlet's quilt into the air. She saw something flutter and fly. When the quilt came to rest on Scarlet's bed, Amber picked up the sheet of paper from where it had fallen on the floor. It wasn't much of a list, just a bold red-lettered heading, too big and bright for Amber to miss.

SCARLET SILK'S STEPS TO CHANGE THE WORLD

Amber might easily have mistaken it for the title of a book except Scarlet walked into the room and said, 'What are you doing with my list?'

Then she remembered that the first item she planned to write on her list was to be nicer to her family. At the same time Scarlet noticed Amber had made her bed, Amber handed her the list.

'Sorry,' they both said at once.

'I just picked it up off the floor,' said Amber.

'Thanks,' said Scarlet. 'And thanks for making my bed.'

She sighed and flopped down onto her perfectly made bed.

'I really am sorry, Amber. I want to change the world but I can't even change myself.'

'Why would you want to do that?' said Amber trying not to be disappointed about Scarlet's bed being messed up. 'Change yourself, I mean. I think you're exactly right the way you are.'

Scarlet looked at her sister. 'Do you really?'

Amber nodded. 'You're pretty and funny and smart and you're. . . interesting.'

'Interesting?'

'Yes. I don't know anyone else who's fifteen and wants to change the world.'

'Hurry girls, the bus is coming,' Annie called.

Scarlet hauled up her holey black tights, stuffed her feet into her laced-up shoes and grabbed her bag with one hand and Amber's hand with the other. Amber looked wistfully back at Scarlet's untidy bed, but there was no time to fix it.

The radio was playing on the bus. The news broadcast had just begun. Anik was waiting at stop seven, outside the Colour Patch Café. The driver pulled the bus in to the kerb as the radio announcer began an interview with someone from the government about sending soldiers to a war overseas.

Over the past two days, the people of other lands had become real to Scarlet. They had jobs, names, families and faces like Anik's or one of his aunties', his uncle's or his grandmother's. The bus brakes squealed, the door slapped open and the queue of passengers stepped up the silver steps.

Then the driver tuned the radio to a music station and Scarlet felt guilty and glad at the same time. She didn't want to hear about soldiers and fighting and she didn't want Anik to hear it either.

But after Social Studies, Scarlet asked Mrs Ogilvy about what she'd heard on the radio news.

'Why is the government sending our soldiers?'

'It's been a long war,' said Mrs Ogilvy. 'There are soldiers there from many countries. Our soldiers are going to help out, that's all. There's nothing for you to worry about, Scarlet.'

'What about the people who live there?' said Scarlet. 'The ordinary people, the families and children? Shouldn't we worry about them?'

'There's nothing you can do about it,' said Mrs Ogilvy, shrugging.

'Yes, there is. My grandmother says there is,' said Scarlet.

'There's no need to be rude, Scarlet,' said Mrs Ogilvy.

'I'm not being rude. I'm just telling you what my grandmother said. She said I can change the world and Nell never lies.'

Mrs Ogilvy had grown up without a grandmother. She had never heard of leftover magic or tried to see the world through someone else's spectacles.

She gave Scarlet lunchtime detention, which was very helpful. By the end of it Scarlet had decided on a small step to change the world. She had declared peace on Cameron's Creek.

Anik wasn't on the bus going home. He went to his Advanced English class instead. Scarlet sat by herself and wondered what Anik would think of her idea. Would he understand? Should she ask him first? Would he be pleased or not? When the bus pulled in to the stop opposite the Colour Patch Café, Scarlet told her sisters she had to talk to Mr Kadri.

'Tell Mama I'll walk home later,' she said.

Mr Kadri was very busy, too busy to stop and talk but never too busy to greet anyone who entered his shop.

'Good afternoon, Miss Crimson,' he said, smiling widely at Scarlet as he rushed by with a tray of tall glasses, ice cubes clinking. Scarlet put a spare apron on over her school uniform, wiped some tables, carried some dishes to the kitchen and even made two raspberry spiders while she waited to speak to Mr Kadri about her big wish and her small step.

Mr Kadri knew how important big wishes are. If you never wished them in the first place, how could they possibly come true? Of course, like everyone, Mr Kadri had wished red-kite kind of wishes, too. A silver-backed brush for his wife's long hair, a holiday by the sea and a paintbrush as fine as a walrus's whisker. But his big wish had taken many years and many small steps to come true.

Mr Kadri had stowed away, hungered and thirsted, lived in fear, was found and fenced in. He waited and waited, then worked all day, wept all night and learnt a language. At last Mr Kadri bought an old shop in Cameron's Creek and painted its walls all the colours of paradise. He called it the Colour Patch Café and sent for his brown-eyed wife and their three curly-haired babies to come and live with him in peace and safety and freedom. But Mr Kadri's wish had grown even bigger. Now he wished those same things for all people.

At last all the customers at the Colour Patch Café had been served and Mr Kadri stopped. In front of him stood one of the colourful daughters of Benjamin Silk, telling him, Kassad Kadri, about her own very big wish. And Mr Kadri was feeling utterly astonished. He clasped his hands together, tipped his head back and gazed towards his upstairs paradise thinking to himself, 'Here is a girl whose life has always been beautiful and peaceful and safe and free and yet her very big wish seems so much like my own.'

And then the girl whose name means red was telling him about her one small step to change the world — her declaration of peace on Cameron's Creek. Mr Kadri closed his eyes and wiped the tears that dribbled from their corners.

Scarlet wasn't sure if this was a good sign. So she asked very quietly, 'Do you think Anik and his family would mind, Mr Kadri?'

'Oh, Miss Crimson,' said Mr Kadri, 'I am weeping tears of joyfulness and I am thinking Anik and his family will be greatly honoured.'

That night, Scarlet cut up all her black tights with pinking shears. When Annie saw what she'd done and asked why, Scarlet said sometimes you had to make sacrifices for the things you believe in.

She told Annie and Ben how she wanted people everywhere to live in peace and how she was planning on changing the world one step at a time. Then she gave them the note from Mrs Ogilvy. Ben and Annie gave Scarlet their blessing to change the world, but asked if she could please try to do it without being rude to people.

Next morning at breakfast, Scarlet was wearing a strip of her sacrificed tights around her arm and a tear-shaped rhinestone stuck to her cheek. She made an announcement to her family that the black armband was a sign of her sadness for all the innocent people affected by war. By wearing a black armband, Scarlet hoped other people would think about them too. It was a small step towards making a wish come true. A wish for wars to end. A wish for peace.

It was also two weeks until Christmas.

10. Black Tights and Band-Aids

After breakfast, Scarlet borrowed Amber's bicycle and went riding with a chocolate box under her arm, her bare legs pumping up and down and her insides doing loop-the-loops. Mr Kadri had agreed to sell her armbands at the Colour Patch Café.

Griffin had released his crickets into the wild, put his chocolate wrapper collection between the pages of *The Comprehensive Illustrated Ornithologist's Bible* and donated his Black Magic chocolate box to Scarlet. Now it was filled with armbands and Indigo had painted a sign on the inside of its lid — *Wishbands: fifty cents each.*

As she neared the café, Scarlet grew more and more nervous. Anik would be there. She wondered if Mr Kadri had remembered to tell him about her plan.

But it wasn't Anik she saw first. It was his grandmother and his two aunties and his one uncle, all standing straight and tall on the grey slate flagstones under the striped awnings and the switched-off neon sign outside Mr Kadri's café. They were waiting for the bus to take them to work at the smallgoods factory. Their heads turned at the sound of Amber's squealing bicycle brakes. They recognised the colourful daughter of Mr Benjamin Silk. Mr Kadri had told them that this girl who made spiders to drink and Anik to smile, also made very big wishes. She was their true friend. They dipped their heads to her and Scarlet dipped hers in return and then Anik came.

'You honour my people,' he said softly. 'My grandmother Mosas, Auntie Shim, Auntie Janda and Uncle Tansil.'

One by one, Anik's family offered their hands and shy smiles to Scarlet. Then the early bus arrived and the aunties and uncle got on and the grandmother stayed and watched and watched as the bus took them away from her.

Scarlet's wishbands were a great success. The Rainbow Girls and Griffin wore one each to school. Amber was especially excited. She was so proud of her interesting sister she stopped off after school and told Elsie all about Scarlet's big wish.

For months, Elsie-from-the-post-office had seen Mr Kadri's friends catching the early bus to the smallgoods factory and she knew Anik's grandmother bounced babies on her knees in the Kadris' upstairs paradise. The quiet people didn't buy stamps or string. They had no words to ask for them, no need for them, no one to send letters or parcels to. And they didn't need a post box with a small black door and a silver key, because no one sent them any letters. Elsie was seventy-two years old and after Amber's visit, she felt slightly disappointed in herself. She had never visited Anik's family and had never wished a wish as big as Scarlet Silk's.

Layla bought a wishband because of John William. She and Griffin once had a dear old friend named Miss Amelie. John William was Miss Amelie's sweetheart. He went away to war and Miss Amelie waited for him until the day she died, but John William never came back. Layla wanted Scarlet's plan to work so that what happened to John William and Miss Amelie would never happen again.

Mr Davis, the bus driver, asked Annie about the wishbands she and Nell were wearing. Then he told them about the olden days when he wasn't much older than Scarlet. He said he'd been sent to jail because he wouldn't fight in a war and he said he'd rather wear one of Scarlet's armbands any day, than a shiny golden medal.

Small things happened at Cameron's Creek that week. Scarlet Silk had lunchtime detention five times for being out of uniform. Elsie put a box of wishbands on the post office counter next to the balls of string and books of stamps.

Bigger things happened, too. Ben used the timber from the old bridge at Gypsy's Bend to build a table. It was so long he had to open the doors at both ends of his shed and his secret men's business wasn't secret anymore.

Scarlet's tights were being worn on the arms of all sorts of people. The Lollipop Lady, Constable Wilson, Mr Davis, Mr Jenkins, Miss Cherry and the preacher from Saint Benedict's Church. But by far the most wishbands were worn by children.

By Friday afternoon, Scarlet had enough money to buy six new pairs of tights and a packet of plasters. She put the plasters on her feet where her shoes rubbed and cut the new tights into armbands.

On Saturday morning, Indigo and Annie set up a silk screen in the studio and printed the flyers Indigo had designed for the next small step in Scarlet's peace plan.

Scarlet rode Amber's bicycle to the charity shop and found a rack of brand new blue T-shirts. They were seventy-five cents each but the lady let Scarlet have eleven for the price of ten because the sleeves were sewn on inside out. That afternoon, while Annie, Perry and Indigo printed a white dove on the front of each T-shirt, Griffin and Layla and the other Rainbow Girls cycled all over Cameron's Creek, poking flyers into letterboxes.

As Christmas drew closer, red-kite kind of wishes seemed less and less important to the people of Cameron's Creek. They didn't think about what gifts they would receive or worry about what they would eat or wonder what to wear. When they met at the post office or the bus stop or the school, they talked about where they could buy more wishbands or discussed the flyers they had found in their letterboxes. And whenever they read the word *peace* on Christmas greeting cards, they thought about children who didn't know what it was like to live in peace.

On Monday during lunchtime detention, Scarlet Silk from the small town of Cameron's Creek began the next part of her plan to change the world. She wrote a letter to the Prime Minister of Australia.

11. The Rearrangement of Mrs Ogilvy's Face

This is the letter Scarlet wrote:

Dear Prime Minister,

My name is Scarlet Silk and I am fifteen years old. I live in a small town called Cameron's Creek with my grandmother, my mother and father, five sisters and two brothers.

My sisters and our friends go to school in the next town because there is no secondary school here. One of my friends is Anik. He has only lived at Cameron's Creek for a few months. He comes on the school bus in the morning and then goes to Advanced English classes after school. Then he teaches what he has learnt to his grandmother, aunties and uncle. They all live together in a flat above the Colour Patch Café. The flat and the café belong to Mr Kadri. It was Mr Kadri who got Anik's family jobs at the Cameron's Creek Smallgoods Factory. Mr Kadri used to work there a long time ago. He knows what it's like to leave everything and everyone you know and love, on the other side of the world. That is why he lets Anik's family live in the flat with him and his wife and three children.

I know this is a long letter and I know you are a busy person, but it is important you get all the facts. The other day when I was going to school on the bus, they said on the radio news you were sending some more soldiers to the country where Anik and his people come from. My Social Studies teacher says there has been fighting there for a long time and people get killed there every day. Not just soldiers, ordinary people. The people in Anik's village are ordinary people. Some are fishermen, some are basket weavers. None of them are soldiers. They have no guns, *but they still get killed. Anik doesn't know what has happened to his parents and sisters. I think it would be a good idea if you didn't send any more soldiers until we find a better way.*

I am not the only one who thinks this. My grandmother, Nell Silk, believes ordinary people like me can change the world. The thing I want to change most of all is for people to stop fighting each other. Ten days ago I declared peace on Cameron's Creek. Since then my family and friends and I have been doing things to spread the word. I have discovered there are a lot of other people like me in Cameron's Creek, who want to change the world. We know it might take a long time, maybe even years, but if we can get enough people to think like us, then there will be no one left to fire guns or drop bombs.

In my family we call wishes that don't matter Red-Kite Wishes. Wishing for peace is not a red-kite kind of wish. It is important. You are an important person and I think you could help us make our wish for peace come true. We have arranged a peace march to be held in Cameron's Creek on Christmas Eve and I would like you to come along.

I don't know if you have ever heard of Cameron's Creek. You will know you have come to the right place when you see a sign that says, 'Welcome to Cameron's Creek, Home of the Big Ham'. We are famous here for the Christmas hams made at the smallgoods factory. They also make sausages and bacon but we are not so famous for them. If you accept my invitation, you might help the people of Cameron's Creek to become famous for something else. We have asked the Daily Beacon *newspaper to send someone along to take photographs of the event.*

I have enclosed your official invitation to our peace march with this letter. Also enclosed is a wishband in case you are unable to attend. I hope you will wear it when you go on official business to England or the United States of America or other overseas places. We want everyone to know the people of Cameron's Creek have declared peace on the whole world.

Yours sincerely,
Scarlet Silk

On the last day of term Scarlet knocked on the staffroom door. Mrs Ogilvy looked through the glass pane in the top of the door. Her eyes took in

Scarlet's bare legs, the rhinestone teardrop on her cheek, the red poem on the pale skin of her arm and her mermaidenly hair spilling free over her shoulders. She opened the door.

'I'd like to make a copy of this letter before I send it away, please,' said Scarlet.

'Wait here,' said Mrs Ogilvy, taking the Prime Minister's letter with her.

Scarlet leaned her back against the grey wall of the corridor and waited. She waited a long time.

Mrs Ogilvy sat down on a hard plastic chair near the copying machine and read Scarlet's letter. Then she tried to remember what kind of girl she had been when she was fifteen years old and it was almost Christmas. And she wished she had been brave enough to ask questions about big things, lucky enough to have a grandmother to tell her she could change the world, wise enough to believe it and bold enough to try.

When she came back with the letter and one warm copy, Mrs Ogilvy's face was rearranged into soft, sad creases and she said, 'I owe you an apology, Scarlet Silk, and I hope your wish comes true.'

12. The Bridge From Gypsy Bend

When Scarlet arrived at the Colour Patch Café on Saturday morning, Mr Kadri was fussing and flapping.

'Oh Miss Crimson,' he said, 'my friends do not wish to be walking in your peace march tomorrow and I am thinking they are afraid.'

'What are they afraid of, Mr Kadri?'

'They will not say, Miss Crimson, but in their

homeland, marching is not permitted. No marching of any kind. I am thinking they are afraid Constable Wilson will be locking them up if they come peace marching with us.'

'Have you told them they'll be safe? Don't they understand? Where is Anik?'

Anik was having an end–of–year celebration with the other people from his Advanced English class.

Scarlet had lived almost every minute of every day of her fifteen years being not afraid of anything. She had not thought this one small step in her plan to change the world could make someone else afraid. But Anik's family had spent most of the last fifteen years being afraid, so how could she tell them they need not be? Even Mr Kadri had faint memories of fear. Scarlet wanted Anik to be there, certain he still had some of the magic he was born with. A child's magic is powerful in any land and language, in war and in peace. It allows them to build palaces from packing crates and make dresses for princesses from rags and tatters. Surely Anik had enough magic left to rub off on his family, just enough for them to find a small pocket of peace, enough to let them feel free to march.

Scarlet put her apron on and wiped tables, washed dishes and waited for Anik to come home from his end-of-year celebration. While she was waiting and wiping, Scarlet thought about all the things still to be done before the march. At home everyone would be busy. Nell would still be baking and Ben... Suddenly Scarlet thought of something that might help Anik's people not to be afraid.

At six o'clock Mrs Ogilvy went to church. The preacher wore a wishband over his crisp white sleeve. At the end of the service he said, 'For twenty-three years I've stood in this church on Christmas Eve and prayed for peace on earth. But this year I've cancelled the Christmas Eve service. Instead I'll be walking in Scarlet Silk's peace march. Judging by the number of black armbands I can see, I'm sure most of you plan to do the same. I'll look forward to seeing you tomorrow. In case there's anyone here who isn't aware of the details, you'll find a flyer in your hymn book explaining everything.'

Mrs Ogilvy tucked the flyer in her handbag, shook hands with the preacher and walked home with bells ringing in her ears. She was feeling fearless and free for the first time in her life.

At dusk the preacher pulled on his old patched jeans and his Cat Stevens T-shirt. He adjusted his leather aviator goggles and fastened the strap of his helmet under his chin, then climbed aboard his Vespa scooter. He had an appointment at the Kingdom of Silk.

Ben's table was sticking out both ends of the shed. The preacher saw it as soon as he pulled up next to the Bedford. It was the longest table he had ever seen. Constable Wilson was standing outside the shed, talking to Anthony Elliott, Layla's daddy, and her big brother Patrick who was practising to be a body builder. A few minutes later Mr Davis arrived with Mr Kadri, Scarlet, Anik and another man. A tall and graceful man with eyes full of secrets. Mr Kadri introduced him to the others. His name was Tansil, Anik's uncle.

Constable Wilson stuck his hand out and said, 'Teddy Wilson's the name. Pleased to meet you, Tansil.'

After everyone had shaken Tansil's hand, the men arranged themselves around Ben's table. Uncle Tansil stood between the policeman and the preacher and grasped the table with all the other men and together they lifted it and carried it slowly towards the dam. Layla and Griffin shouted directions and encouragement from the tree house. The men sweated and strained and stopped and started and at last set the table down on the grass near the Cox's Orange Pippin.

Then the Rainbow Girls came down from the house, carrying plates piled high with watermelon smiles and fruit salad ice blocks on sticks. Nell and Annie brought trays of tumblers and jugs of juice and Superman skipped along behind them all, singing superhero songs to his shadow, Blue.

On that hot summer evening before the day of the peace march, Ben's helpers ate and drank and laughed and listened while Ben told the true tale of the table. For Uncle Tansil's sake he told things the others already knew and Anik explained the words his uncle didn't understand. Ben salvaged used timber and made it into chairs and chests, cribs and cradles, banisters and bookcases, pigeon holes and pirate's legs and rolling pins or other things and sometimes almost everything.

'Remember the old bridge at Gypsy Bend?' said Ben prodding at their memories.

Some of the other men nodded.

'Well, they replaced it with a steel bridge last year, so I brought the timber from the old one here. I wanted to use it for something special, but I couldn't think what, so I kept it in the shed. When Scarlet started talking about her wish for peace it got me thinking about how bridges bring people together. And I suddenly realised that if you turn a bridge into a table, it does much the same thing. So I decided to use the timber from the bridge at Gypsy Bend to make a table, the biggest table I could, to bring as many people together as I could. Thanks everyone for helping me shift it. We're planning to serve supper on it tomorrow night after the peace march. You're all invited.'

Constable Wilson offered Mr Kadri, Anik and Uncle Tansil a ride back to the Colour Patch Café in his police car. He didn't have a gun and he didn't search them or put handcuffs on them. He just said, 'In you get.'

Mr Kadri talked almost all the way home.

'Mr Benjamin Silk is a very good man, wouldn't you say, Tansil? He has many, many beautiful children and then he brings home another one who is not altogether his. The little one in his magical costume, Superiorman. Benjamin is also taking care of his mother and his beautiful wife. And now he is inviting us all to come again to his house to make celebrations after Miss Crimson's marching. We are indeed fortunate, Tansil, to have such a good neighbour as Benjamin Silk.'

As they drew up outside the Colour Patch Cafe, Anik said, 'Constable Wilson, do we have your permission to march in peace tomorrow?'

Constable Wilson turned around in his seat and looked at Tansil and Anik and Mr Kadri all sitting in the back with questions in their eyes.

'Permission?' he said. 'This is the most exciting thing to happen in Cameron's Creek for years. I'll be in the front row. You can march next to me if you like!'

The café's neon sign blinked on and all the colours of paradise flooded through the window and onto Uncle Tansil's smiling face.

13. Plum Puddings and Paper Moons

The starting line for the march was outside the Colour Patch Café. Not many cars drove down the High Street at that hour of the evening, because the café closed at half-past six and the march didn't start until eight o'clock. But Constable Wilson put orange witches' hats and detour signs at both ends of the High Street to make everything look official.

Then he took off his policeman's jacket and put on one of Scarlet's screen-printed T-shirts. It was the extra, extra large one, and even so, the white dove was slightly stretched. But inside that T-shirt was Constable Teddy Wilson who was Katie's daddy, and a very good man. And besides, as everyone knows, a chubby dove is as much a symbol of peace as a skinny one.

It was more a meander than a march. More a celebration than a demonstration. A celebration of the right to speak about things you think are wrong. It was also a thanksgiving for people who are brave enough to make big wishes.

Mr Jenkins led the way, playing the bagpipes. He'd once been a member of the Clan Macleod Highland Pipe band. He wore a kilt in those days and his Juliette fell in love with him because he had such nice legs. But it was too hot for pleated skirts on the evening of the march so Mr Jenkins just wore his tartan socks, and his sporran over his shorts. He played a tune called 'Amazing Grace' three times over because it had been Juliette's favourite song and was the only one he could remember by heart.

Perry Angel marched next to his friend Jenkins, beating his soup-pot snare drum with wooden spoons. Ben had loaned him a fur hat with a fox's tail that Nell made for him when he was Perry's age. And Annie had coaxed the echidna out of Perry's gumboot with some worms from Nell's worm farm. Perry looked very smart in his fur hat and gumboots with his Superman cape flying out behind him. Blue was the band's mascot and walked between Mr Jenkins and Perry with a 'P for peace' sign around his neck.

Behind the band came the banner-bearers. Annie had made an old sheet into a banner with the words *We've Declared Peace on the World* printed across it in blue. She threaded Nell's brass curtain rods through the seams at each end and Scarlet and Anik carried it between them.

After the banner-bearers walked Mr and Mrs Kadri and Grandmother Mosas pushing toddlers in strollers, then Auntie Shim, Auntie Janda and Uncle

Tansil proudly wearing new blue T-shirts printed with white doves. In their hearts they carried the sadness of things lost: parents, children, brothers, sisters, limbs and lives and land. But with each small step they took, Anik and his family thought of all the things they had found: friendship, food, shelter, safety, the right to march in peace and a colourful girl called Scarlet Silk.

Scarlet had spent the rest of her wishband

money and some of her pay from her Saturday job on candles and Mr Kadri gave her paper cups to put them in, enough cups and candles for all the marchers to carry one.

They walked as far as the sports ground behind Saint Benedict's where they put their coffee-cup candles on the ground and joined hands. Old hands with young hands, dark with pale, small with large and rough with smooth in a long unbroken chain

around the football field. Some people sang, others read or recited poems, some said their thankful thoughts out loud and others closed their eyes and made deep and silent wishes. Then the preacher rang the church bell and the children set white balloons free. They floated into the darkening heavenlies as silently as peace does when war ends.

Soon after, Mr Davis drove his bus through the gates in a cloud of dust and Ben climbed up on the monkey bars with a megaphone. First he thanked everyone for coming and then he said, 'Refreshments will be served at the Kingdom of Silk. We'd love you all to come. For those of you who don't have transport and can't walk so far, Mr Davis has kindly offered to take you there in his bus.'

Elsie-from-the-post-office was the first to board the bus. She knew the Silk Road well. There wasn't much more than a lick of tar on it now and she was certain all those loose red pebbles would jam the wheels of her walking frame. Besides, she wanted to have a chat with Mr Jenkins. She was sure he wouldn't be intending to carry his bagpipes so far on such a hot night.

The journey from the sportsground to the Kingdom of Silk was another procession. Some people walked, others rode bicycles or drove cars and the preacher rode his Vespa. People came with folding chairs or picnic rugs and many brought food to share.

Ben cooked pizzas-to-order and Amber's heart-shaped Armenian Love Cakes were a huge success. So were Auntie Ruby's rumless rum balls. Elsie ate three. Then she brushed the crumbs off her cornflower-

blue cardigan with a lace handkerchief and said she'd better not have any more in case she got tipsy. And before Amber had time to explain that the rum balls were as fake as pirate's moustaches, Elsie stood up and wobbled her way across to the bridge from Gypsy's Bend for a nice strong cup of tea.

When supper was over, Griffin and Layla climbed up on the haystack and lay on their backs watching the stars burn. Perry curled up in Annie's arms. He'd taken off his cape and his gumboots and Ben's fur hat. There was no need for a superhero tonight and he was no longer Drum Major. He was simply Perry Angel. He knew now that Perry Angel was a good thing to be and the Kingdom of Silk was in safe hands. His beautiful, scary, interesting teenage sister Scarlet had declared peace on the world.

Scarlet and Anik sat on the raft, full of magic and rum balls. Coffee-cup candles drifted beside them on the to-ings and fro-ings of the tides as they navigated the dark canals of Venice and glided silently beneath the Bridge of Sighs.

Being fifteen wasn't so bad, Scarlet thought. You could be very brave and slightly wise but sometimes scared. When you were angry, loud or mean, you could be forgiven. It was okay to agree or disagree. And you could fight war with peace and fall a tiny bit in love. Scarlet had been and done all of the above but best of all she had made her grandmother proud.

Nell reclined on her deckchair under the Cox's

Orange Pippin. Voices drifted across the dam. A breath of wind wrinkled the water and rustled the paper chain that hugged the appled boughs. Candles flickered, lanterns danced, an angel face floated in the dark and Nell knew Tishkin was there.

Her thoughts flew to the deep and silent wish that all the Silks had wished and to the *little more as well* that Layla had written in her journal. Then to a line from her favourite poem: *A time to be born and a time to die*. And a pure and perfect thought was born. Nell knew, as surely as day follows night, that when it was her time, she wasn't going anywhere. Like Tishkin she would stay, forever in the wind and the soil and the sky at the Kingdom of Silk. She smiled in the darkness and promised herself she wouldn't forget to tell Layla and Griffin in the morning.

At five minutes to twelve, Ben took out his mouth organ and played the preacher's favourite tune, 'Morning Has Broken', and Annie sang. Mr and Mrs Elliott danced under the curtsying boughs of the Cox's Orange Pippin and Layla made a deep and silent wish that every Christmas could be like this one.

Then someone called out.

'It's midnight! It's Christmas Day!'

Annie shook Nell gently.

'It's time,' she said and together they walked up
to the kitchen.

The Prime Minister didn't come to Scarlet's peace
march, but three hundred and seventeen other
people did, which was a lot of people for a small
town like Cameron's Creek. It was almost all the
people.

Not everyone was from Cameron's Creek. Melody
was there with three small girls and so was Sunday
Lee. But there was enough of Nell's leftover-on-
purpose plum pudding for everyone to have a slice.
On each plate beside the pudding was a small paper
doily. In the centre, written in red, was Scarlet's wish:
Peace on Earth. If you held the doily against the sky
it looked almost exactly like a moon.

The *Daily Beacon* called the peace march a triumph and printed a photograph of Scarlet on the front page. Underneath it said: *Miss Scarlet Silk is hopeful that by next year, people in towns and cities all over the world will follow the example of the people of Cameron's Creek and declare peace on war.*

A note from Glenda

People often ask me where I get inspiration from. So I thought I'd share some secrets with you. I hope they will help you to discover where I got some of the ideas for things I've written about in *Plum Puddings and Paper Moons*.

When I was a little girl in primary school, the milkman used to deliver milk to the school in small glass bottles with lids made of silver foil. We used to wash the lids and save them up to make Christmas decorations at the end of the year.

My younger sister and I used to love making wishes, especially when it came close to Christmas. But my parents didn't have a lot of money and often we didn't get what we wished for. Sometimes my dad would assemble bicycles from bits and pieces of other bikes. Then he'd paint them and decorate them with transfers. My mum would make beautiful rag dolls with scraps of fabric left over from dresses she'd sewn for us. So even when our red-kite kind of wishes didn't come true, we were just as happy with our rag dolls and second-hand bicycles.

I used to ride my bicycle to school and on the way home I'd call in to the post office to collect our mail. The people who ran the post office were Mr and Mrs Rasmussen.

I left school just before I turned sixteen and one of the first things I bought when I got my pay was a white cake tin with cornflowers painted on it. I bought it for my nana.

In that small country town where I was born and grew up, there was a factory that preserved meats. A lot of the people who lived in my town worked in this factory. It is still there today and now people who are refugees from other lands have come to live in the town and many work at the factory.

A few years ago, I heard on the news and read in the papers that soldiers from Australia were going to a war in a far away land. Because of this some people in our town arranged a peace march. We all walked up the main street holding candles until we got to the sports ground behind the school. We held hands there and talked and sang and wished that we could change the world. Afterwards we had supper. A lady called Elsie gave me a piece of cake. She said it was called Armenian Love Cake. It seemed right to me to be sitting on the grass under the starry sky, eating cake that came from a recipe from a land far away and wondering how we could change the world. The cake was so delicious that I asked Elsie for the recipe so I could make it myself. And now I'm passing it on to you. Perhaps you could ask an adult to help you make it.

Armenian Love Cake

2 cups plain flour
2 teaspoons baking powder
1 cup brown sugar
A pinch of salt
125 grams butter, chopped
1 teaspoon baking soda
1 cup milk
1 egg, lightly beaten
1 teaspoon freshly grated nutmeg
½ cup roughly chopped golden walnuts

Pre-heat the oven to 180°C.

Line a cake tin with baking paper. (I like to use a heart-shaped tin, but any kind will do.)

Sift the flour, baking powder, brown sugar and salt into a large bowl. Rub the butter into the dry ingredients with your fingertips until the mixture is crumbly. Place half of this mixture in the cake tin.

In a separate bowl, dissolve the baking soda in the milk, then add the egg and nutmeg. Combine the remaining dry mixture with the wet ingredients and mix thoroughly. Pour this on top of the dry mixture in your cake tin. Cover the top with the chopped walnuts.

Bake for about one hour. You can test to see if it is cooked by inserting a skewer. If the skewer comes out clean, the cake is cooked.

When cooked, remove the cake from oven and leave in the tin for about 10 minutes before turning out onto a cooling rack. Serve warm or cold.

Best shared with friends and eaten in peace.